At This Very Minute

Kathleen Rice Bowers

Illustrated by Linda Shute

LITTLE, BROWN AND COMPANY
BOSTON   TORONTO

FIRST EDITION

Library of Congress Cataloging in Publication Data

Bowers, Kathleen Rice.
  At this very minute.

  Summary: While a child is about to be tucked
snugly into bed, many different activities are
taking place all over the world.
  [1. Bedtime—Fiction] I. Shute, Linda, ill.
II. Title.
PZ7.B6765At 1983   [E]   82-4712
ISBN 0-316-10400-0
ISBN 0-316-10401-9 (pbk.)

AHS

Published simultaneously in Canada
by Little, Brown and Company (Canada) Limited

PRINTED IN THE UNITED STATES OF AMERICA

To those who've shared
appreciation and encouragement,
especially
Kay Jones
and her sister,
Helen Clayton.

K. R. B.

To my parents,
Ann and Melvin McElhiney,
and their love
for children around the world.

L. M. S.

At This Very Minute

Somewhere in this town,
at this very minute,
somebody is sneezing. (God bless you, somebody.)

Somewhere in this town,
a baby is having her diaper changed.
Someone else is being kissed.

Someone's going to the kitchen to get a snack.
At this very minute,
someone's washing his hands.

Somewhere in this town a light is going off.
And right now another light is going on.

Somewhere else in this big country of ours,
at this very minute,
a lazy cow is munching grass.
Somewhere
    a bicycle has been left out in the rain,
    a dog is scratching at the back door,
    a bag lady sits on a park bench to rest awhile.
    Beside her are two shopping bags
    that hold everything she owns.

Somewhere in the country, in a dark cellar corner,
a cat catches a mouse.   POUNCE!   *Purrrrr.*

Somewhere someone just got an idea
about how to solve a problem:
    to fix a tractor
    to heal a sick child
    to mend hurt feelings.

11

Somewhere in the land,
at this very moment,
a paperboy rides his bike down the street,
with a barking dog at his heels.
The boy kicks the dog away,
and throws the evening news toward someone's front door.
All the houses on the street look the same on the outside,
but inside there are many different people
doing many different things.

While you are looking at this page,
people are reading newspapers, all across the country —
sitting in the kitchen, wearing a bathrobe,
sipping coffee,

on a subway, elbow to elbow,
on a cable car,
at the desk of the night watchman,
in the big office building downtown.

In some city in this land,
someone is climbing out of the rain,
into a taxicab.
At the same time, throughout the land,
people watch someone on TV
mop up a puddle of milk
with a paper towel.

Right now, a grandmother sits by the phone,
waiting for it to ring.
Somewhere a boy is looking at the front door,
knowing that any minute Daddy will be home.

In another city, a family has just arrived.

They have left their home in a faraway land.

Tonight they are tired,

and crying inside for the places

and people they love, that they will never see again,

wondering whom to trust.

They cannot speak our language.

Suddenly they smile together.

Auntie has come to meet them!

They hug her, all at once, and cry happy tears.

She has brought presents.

Blocks for the baby, books for sister,

and clothes for everyone.

Baby's blocks have something different on each side.

So does the world.

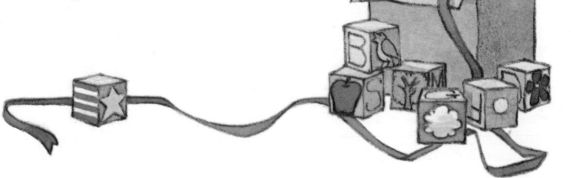

17

On the other side of the world,
at this very minute, a house is being built.
Somewhere in the world, at this very minute,
it's already tomorrow!

Somewhere a baby is taking its first look
and crying its first cry.
Someone is swimming all the way out
to the raft in the pond
for the very first time.

In a store,
someone looks at the price,
counts some coins in his hand,
shakes his head,
puts the coins back in his pocket,
and walks away.

Under an oak tree
a boy and a girl have found some twigs.
Together they build an imaginary world,
which seems far more real than any other,
at this very minute.

Someone is picking a flower for a special friend.
Someone is setting a flower arrangement on a banquet table,
beneath a crystal chandelier.

Far away,
someone is eating a dinner of rice,
with chopsticks.
While someone else, who had no dinner tonight,
is telling his tummy to be quiet so he can get some sleep.

Somewhere,
workers are picking lettuce
beneath a sun so hot
their backs shine with sweat.

While, at the very same minute,
someplace else,
a snowplow is clearing someone's street.

On our street,
at this very minute,
it is dark.
Someone looks through a window
for the moon.

26

And at this very minute
someone is about to be tucked snugly into bed

and kissed goodnight

to sleep soundly all night long.